JOURNEY INTO FRIENDS

KAVYA VISALIRAM

I dedicate this book to my Best Friend " Tejaswi"

The persons who think they are unworthy to chase anything in their life then I dedicate this book to them.

Unfortunately, few months back even I felt the same as I am unworthy to chase my dream so I fought with myself without hurting anyone and I bounced back to this and now my writings are in your hand. To those who says I'm unworthy - this is my answer "I MADE MY DREAMS, THIS IS ME"

I believe that nobody is unworthy to chase their dreams....

Contents

Preface

"JOURNEY INTO FRIENDS" is a book which says that nobody is unworthy to chase their dreams and everybody has the ability to chase their dreams. It is also about an anxiety girl who shows her interest in knowing more things and also a girl who chases her dreams and gives more preferences to relationship and friendship. This book even make you know what fantasies you can have in your life.

Acknowledgements

"JOURNEY INTO FRIENDS" is a dream book of the a girl who feels herself as unworthy to chase her dreams in this competitive world. " Deepest thanks to the people who helped me in making my dream in front of you. Achieving a dream without any second person is really very difficult to achieve, poetic souls publications helped me in getting my writings infront of you.

ONE

There is a girl named Smithi, who is playing with her best friend chaitra in a beautiful nursery.

There bonding is just like they cannot live without each other. Smithi is very possessive towards chaitra. Smithi doesn't allow any other girl to be with chaitra. Smithi is very good artist, calm and silent in her convent whereas chaitra is very dare and dashing girl. There were no secrets in between them. Smithi shares everything with chaitra and chaitra shares everything with smithi. Both were very active during their classes time and both are the toppers in their class. Now both are studying last grade in their convent, both decided to go to convent a bit early to cover extra topics from their syllabus.

Unexpectedly on one day, smithi gets a love proposal from her friend Abhiram infront of whole class. She doesn't like abhiram's behavior towards her. Smithi rejected his proposal infront of whole class. Firstly, abhiram feels sad as she rejected him. But secondly, he gets angry on smithi's way of rejection. So, abhiram decides to make smithi feel guilt infront of whole class. Abhiram thinks of an evil plan which makes smithi feel guilt infront of whole class. Chaitra gets the gossips about the abhiram's evil plan towards smithi. Chaitra decides to warn abhiram without knowing to smithi. On the next day, chaitra waits for the turn to speak with abhiram. When smithi leaves the place, firstly chaitra asked abhiram to give her two minutes to speak about chaitra. As abhiram says "OK", chaitra says to abhiram that not to disturb smithi by his useless schemes or plans. Then abhiram gets shock and he thinks " how come chaitra came to know about it ?". When chaitra says this to abhiram then he realizes his mistake and he shares his feeling towards sruthi. He says, he was loving her since 3 years. He even shares that he imagined an imaginary life with smithi to chaitra. While he was telling about smithi to chaitra, he becomes little emotional. Then chaitra goes near to abhiram and she controls him from getting emotional.

As chaitra understands his emotion towards smithi, she started telling about smithi character - "Her world is so small, she is too introvert towards her feelings and all know that she is over-possessive towards me, she is very fear of losing people in her life so that's the reason behind as she is not close to more people". When chaitra says about smithi to him, he understands her from his side. On that night, abhiram feels guilt of his thinking level towards smithi , so he decides to ask her apologizing about his behavior. The next day, as abhiram decides to say sorry to smithi, he is waiting for his turn meanwhile smithi and chaitra passes over him. Then Abhiram stops smithi by his hand, and he apologizes her by lying his head down.

Smithi accepts his sorry and she immediately leaves that place by taking chaitra along with her. Meanwhile chaitra feel very happy by abhiram's words and his maturity thinking about smithi's opinions by respecting her feelings. Later chaitra says to abhiram that he too gets a good life sharing partner, then abhiram blushes. But eventhough abhiram didn't stop loving smithi, but he had just stopped showing that love to her on respecting her feelings.

Later smithi gets a doubt that how come he feels sorry to me without any third person interference between us, then immediately chaitra gets strike over smithi's mind. As chaitra is very dare and dashing friend to smithi, she goes to chaitra and asks her whether she has spoken to abhiram about her. Chaitra stays quite and tries to divert the topic. Smithi seriously questions chaitra about abhiram, even though she didn't answer and tries to crack a joke. Then smithi says "If you didn't answer my question, then this will be the last day for both of us". Then Chaitra says 'yes' to smithi and she explains the complete conversation with abhiram. Then smithi becomes dull then meanwhile chaitra goes near to smithi and apologizes for her mistake. Then smithi slaps chaitra as she is apologizing.

《 SMITHI HUGS CHAITRA 》

Smithi feels little emotional and she feels thankful to chaitra as understanding her situation even without sharing with her. Then chaitra says even she is also happy and the reason is abhiram because she didn't expect that he would understand smithi so early by her words. When Chaitra says these words both looks at there faces and smiles and started returning to their homes. Both goes to their home and smithi is a bit fear of her exams. Smithi gets an idea of combine study for exams. Smithi asks chaitra's father to send chaitra to her home for their combine study, chaitra's father accepts to smithi words and he says to take along with her for few days. Chaitra is super happy as she is going to be with smithi all time. Smithi's parents heartily welcomes chaitra to their home. Chaitra's parents feel happy as smithi's parents are taking a good look over chaitra.

On one fine evening while returning from convent, when smithi and chaitra are crossing chaitra's home then they observe many people infront of their home. Both rushes into home in a hurry mode.

They see chaitra's mother lyed on the floor. Chaitra is in shock. And the Remaining Family members tries to explain the situation how the situation happened. Chaitra is unable to believe that her mother is no more. Chaitra becomes over wept by seeing her mother and everyone are trying to control Chaitra. Chaitra losses her control and becomes unconscious. Chaitra is admitted in hospital and the doctor says she is mentally very disturbed and she has gone into depression. After few days, smithi's parents discharges chaitra and takes her to their home . When smithi takes chaitra to her room then suddenly chaitra hugs smithi and she becomes over wept. Chaitra started sharing her emotional moments about her mother. Chaitra stopped going to her convent. After few days, smithi mother convinces chaitra to go to convent as their board exams timetable is scheduled. Chaita says OK to smithi's mother. Smithi is happy as chaitra decides to go to convent.

Both are doing well in their exams. After few months both passed of their convent with highest percentage. All the family members are happy with their children first success. Smithi's father thinks to send them far from the city for their higher education. Smithi's father is very strict towards their children future. Smithi's father shares his opinion with chaitra's father and convinces him to send his daughter along with smithi for there better future.

Chaitra's father thinks a while as now-a-days she is coming out of her depression world and later he obeys to smithi's father for sending his daughter. Smithi's father returns home, he sees his wife is very happy by seeing smithi and chaitra photos in the newspaper. And she shows that news paper to

him with lots of happiness in her eyes. After smithi's father sees the newspaper, he makes his wife sit beside him and he says that he wishes to join them far from the city to give them better future. After hearing that she becomes silent, when he asks for her reply then she says " it is OK to send them as you are saying they get a bright future but how come we can leave them alone and that too far from us". Meanwhile chaitra's father Comes in the middle of their conversation and he says "we have to do that as they get a bright and unstruggled future". Then they three feel very low as they have to send their children to hostel.

When smithi and chaitra returns back home, they see there parents were sad. Both questions their parents for the reason behind their sadness. Parents makes them to sit beside them. Smithi again questions them the reason behind their silence. Smithi's father started telling his idea as they

are going to send them to hostel for next level academic study. After he finishes telling his idea to them, then they becomes silent and they slowly moves to their bedroom. Both thinks about the conversation they had with parents. Chaitra thinks of an idea and goes closer to smithi to share and she says " listen, our parents are sending us for our future and if we do this now then we both can lead the happy future", when smithi listens to chaitra's words then she too felt the same and decides to go to hostel. On the next day, smithi and chaitra goes to their parents and they says that they are ready to go to hostel. Parents feel very happy that they have obeyed to their words. Smithi's father proceeds with further arrangements in sending their children to hostel. Everybody in the family are happy and that happiness can be seen in their eyes. Smithi and

chaitra are also very happy. Smithi draws the happy faces of their family. Both smithi and chaitra pack their belongings needed for them. While both are leaving home, smithi's mother cries as both the children were leaving them. Smithi and chaitra hugs mother and says her to send them happily. While both are leaving home, both are a bit sad to be far from their family.

Both started their hostel life happily. After few days smithi feels low as she is missing her mother, chaitra gives strength to smithi, to be strong. After few hours smithi feels normal and she goes back to her normal work. But deep inside chaitra becomes very weak as she is badly missing her mother and father. Smithi notices this and controls chaitra by hugging her. A girl named pinky, comes near to chaitra and controls her along with smithi.

After few months, they both made many friends. Pinky is the common friend to both smithi and chaitra. But pinky feels chaitra as her best friend when compared to smithi. As we already know that smithi is over possessive towards chaitra, so she doesn't like pinky.

Smithi shows her possessiveness infront of pinky as she should know the bonding between smithi and chaitra. Chaitra notices smithi possessive nature infront of pinky. Chaitra smiles for her childish activity. At that night chaitra speaks to smithi that she is behaving very childish infront of pinky. Chaitra continuously laughs by imagining her past childish behavior infront of pinky. Then smithi says – " You just belongs to only me and I am not going to share you with anyone and also no other person is important when compared to you". Chaitra hugs smithi and says that she is very lucky to have smithi in her life.

Both smiles by looking at each other. Smithi gets laugh by imagining her childish behavior infront of pinky. From next day, smithi started being normal infront of pinky. Months passes, they finished their

final exam and both performed very well in their exams. Both are happy as they are going to their home. They started packing all their luggage meanwhile pinky comes to meet smithi and chaitra, she says goodbye to both of them. Then smithi goes towards pinky and she says "sorry, if I hurt you anytime". Pinky says no and she hugs both smithi and chaitra and says goodbye to them. When their packing had come to an end, smithi books a cab for both of them to go to railway station. When the cab arrives then both turned back and sees their college. After getting into cab they feels very high as they are going to meet their parents after two years. Both moves in a cab but unexpectedly the cab gets hit by a heavy loaded truck and the people in the cab (smithi, chaitra, driver) gets heavily injured and they have gone into unconscious state. After sometime the surrounding people in that area observes the accident and they made call to the ambulance and admitted them in the hospital. The hospital people made call to their respective parents and informed them about the accident and asked them to come urgently as it became case.

When both parents received call from hospital, the situation of parents was like they almost lost their strength and the mother keeps over wept. They started their journey to hospital. Meanwhile smithi and chaitra treatment was started. Smithi face got completely damaged due to car broken window glass and chaitra is not responding to the doctor's treatment. The parents reaches hospital in a hurry state. They becomes over wept by seeing their children on the bed. When the parents ask doctor about their children situation, then the doctor thinks how to explain the situation of smithi and chaitra to their parents. Then the doctor finally says that smithi needs a plastic surgery to her face as her face is completely damaged due to car broken window glass pieces. And doctor slowly says that chaitra is not responding to any of there treatment. Later, the

nurse comes out of the doctor cabin and says to parents that doctor wants to discuss about smithi's surgery. Then the parents went inside and the doctor says that smithi need a perfect face to set for her plastic surgery. Parents asks what's the next step to proceed. Doctor says he will inform about it and the parents leave the cabin. Later doctor goes near to smithi's parents and says that he got a face which they can proceed to further surgery. When the doctor leaves the parents then a couple comes near to smithi's parents by crying and says to take a well care about their daughter and they leaves that place. Smithi's parents doesn't understand about whom and what they are talking about.

<<*HOURS PASSES*>>

Doctor comes out the ward and confirms that chaitra is no more. Parents were in completely shock and in deep depression meanwhile chaitra body is passing through them in stretcher. Chaitra's father

couldn't control his emotions and becomes overwept by catching his daughter body. On the other side, smithi surgery was started. Chaitra's father takes chaitra body and says that he goes far from the city because he cannot live with chaitra's memories in that old house. Smithi's are in tension about chaitra and in deep pain as chaitra is no more with them.

<<*SURGERY WAS SUCCESSFUL*>>

Smithi is in operation theatre meanwhile doctor goes to smithi's parents and coveys them that operation is successful and no need to worry about smithi. Doctor says that smithi will be shifted to general ward within 48 hours, then the take a relief breathe and they become thankful to the doctor. Smithi's parents goes near to the operation ward and watches smithi by standing at the door.

<<AFTER 48 HOURS>>

Smithi is shifted to general ward and she tries to open her eyes and watches doctor. Smithi parents were happy as she is becoming normal but inside they were literally thinking about how to convey her about chaitra. The doctor says to smithi that now she is perfectly alright and the doctor allows her parents to watch smithi. Smithi's parents get surprise by watching smithi. Doctor asks the nurse to pass the

mirror and the doctor passes the mirror to smithi, smithi watches her face in the mirror and gets surprises about the change over in her face. Smithi asks about chaitra, smithi parents feel tensed and tries to cover the situation. Smithi overthinks about chaitra when her parents are not replying. Smithi's father try to convey her about chaitra and goes closer to smithi and says about chaitra to her.

<<SMITHI IS SHOCKED>>

Smithi is unwilling to accept her father's words about chaitra. She thinks of her memories with chaitra. She is not even willing to cry and couldn't imagine the chaitra is no more. Doctor says to give rest to smithi and takes her parents out along with him. Smithi overthinks about chaitra and silently sits at one corner of her room. Even the days passes, smithi is not willing to overcome herself from chaitra memories.

<<AFTER FEW DAYS>>

Smithi is discharged, parents are taking her to home. Even while going to home, their vehicle passes over the places where chaitra and smithi used to spend their time. Smithi suddenly stops their vehicle, continuosly watch those places and rememorize all their memories. Parents take smithi to home. Smithi moves to her bedroom, watches chaitra photo flame and burst out her cry and cries loudly. Parents try to control smithi but she overcries loudly by watching chaitra's photo. Later, after

hours, smithi falls asleep by holding chaitra's photo in her hands. Days passes, smithi becomes very silent and she doesn't speak to anyone. Even She is

not willing to share her feelings with parents. smithi always sits infront of mirror and thinks about her face whose face might that be. Smithi losses her

interest in everything and even she is not interested in going out . Smithi's parents worries about smithi by noticing her behaviour. Smithi's father takes smithi out to create her new weather. While smithi

and her father were out, smithi's mother makes a call to her husband and says that somebody has arrived home and wants to talks to us. Smithi and her father goes back to home they notice a wife and

husband sittings on sofa and smithi's mother is sitting opposite to them. Both the stangers (wife and husband) get suprises by seeing smithi. Smithi's father says smithi to go inside her bedroom and her father sits beside his wife. Smithi's father remembers that he had seen them in crying at hospital. Smithi's father ask them the reason behind their appeerence to arrive home. The husband tries to speak but his wife started crying and he controls his wife and he says whatever the face hoe smithis is having is his daughter's face, Janu. He says that he lost his daughter due to brain cancer. Smithi's father goes and sit beside janu's father and controls him from being emotional. Smithi's parents be very thankful and says that they will never forget the help made by them. Janu's father says that janu is the only daughter to them. With the loss of janu they were not in a good mood and couldn't concentrate on any other work. Janu's mother says that by seeing the face like alive. Janu's parents requests smithi's parents to take them along to their home and make smithi also be with them. Janu's parents thinks that by letting smithi and is still alive with them. Smith's parents doesn't like the thought of going to their house. Janu's parents requests them and tries to convince. Smithi's parents doesn't like that thought and doesn't obey to them. Janu's parents says that smithi might be happy if she goes there. Smithi's father says to his wife that if they could change place then smithi may be fee and happy. Smithi's father convinces himself and he calls smithi out and says her about janu and they ask aboout her opinion. Smithi leaves her opinion to her parents and she goes inside. Smithi's parents then obeys to janu's parents words the entire family shifted to janu's Home.

Smithi feels like new home, new weather and everything was completely new to her. Smithi smiles and roams whole house by obeserving everything. Smithi's parents feel happy seeing smithi smile after many days. Janu's parents watches smithi smiling and feel like their daughter is alive and staying with them. Then smithi goes to janu's bed room and see's all the photo frames f her and she searches for album to see more photos. Smthi takes one photo frame and goes infront of mirror and compares herself in

the mirror. By seeing janu's photo album, she is very excited to know more aout janu. Smithi keeps chaitra's photo beside of janu's photo and lights the candle and keeps silent and she thinks silent and she thinks of chaitra and her memories. Smithi set few of her things in janu room and then smithi finds a diary

which is written by janu. When smithi opens her diary mostly filled with the name ANAND. smithi feels like who is that man and she is very eager to know who might be he ? and what might be the relation between them ? smithi even finds many of janu's mature thoughts and she was very excited to know more about janu. Smithi didn't say or ask anything about janu to their parents. Janu's parents goes to smithi and says to be free like their home and advises her to use janu's things and clothes.

<< *AFTER FEW WEEKS* >>

Smithi's parents thinks that smithi is gradually becoming normal so they think's to join her in graduation. So her father searched for best graduation college and joins her in that college in a week, smithi college was started, she started going to new college in a very nervous way. When smithi sits in her classroom, everybody is shocked. Smithi felt more nervous when everybody is watching her. Nobody is not interacting with smithi even if she try to talk them.

‹‹ *EVERYBODY GOSSIPS* ››

Smithi thinks what wrong in her when everybody gossiping, smithi heard janu name and she turned to them then everybody shocks by smithi's turn. A girl comes near to smithi and calls her by janu's name. Then smithi confuses how come they know janu? smithi slowly says that she is not janu iam smithi. And smithi says everything what happened to her till then. Everybody feel surprises and tries to interact with smithi. Mostly everybody calls smithi by janu's name. Even many of her lecturer's confuses by seeing smithi as janu in college again. Smithi goes back to her home says everything that what happened to her in college. Smithi's father says to smithi to say, if anything goes wrong to her in life. Smithi obeys to her father's words and goes inside her bedroom, stands infront of mirror and speaks to face asks who is she and what's her story might be? she thinks whome to ask about janu, she gets idea to ask janu's parents but she stops because while telling they might become more emotional and that's not right manner to ask. Smithi thinks and she goes to her bed. On the next day, smithi is very excited to go to college to find any other way to know about janu. Smithi is slowly knowing about janu everybody said janu is very innocent and creative girl in her academic year and even janu won many awards and medals for her researches.

Smithi feels very inspirational by listening about janu's life but she didn't know who is that anand and she couldn't find anand anywhere in her classroom. Smithi thinks that she is knowing everything about janu but couldn't find that anand. Smithi again opens janu diary to know about anand but she could find only her researches and she could only find the name anand but no other information is found about him. Smithi thinks that who is anand? what might be the relation between anand and janu?

Days passes, smithi knows everything about janu but she couldn't find who might anand be in janu's life? At one cold night, smithi goes to shop to buy groceries then a boy continuosly watches her with reddish eyes filled with tears. Smithi didn't understand who might is he? she doesn't think of him guy follows smithi 10 feet away from her.

Smithi don't understand why is he following her. Smithi stops at one place and questioned him what's the reason behind to follow her. Then he asked how did you come back janu? then smithi understands that he is following for janu not for her. Smithi asks

him, who is he? and why to follow? then he introduces his name as anand. Smithi turns suddenly towards him and conforms is he really anand or not. Anand conforms his name to smithi. Smithi observes that anand is thinking her as his janu. Smithi says him that she is not janu and she says everything. Anand eyes are just like reddish eyes filled with tears by seeing janu again. Smithi questions anand, what is the relation between him and janu? he says if janu

might be alive now now then in future janu and anand will get marry, but unknowing everything has changed within few months.

<< *ANAND BURST OUT HIS CRY* >>

Smithi controls his emotions, then smithi understood the relation between anand and janu. Anand slowly share his complete love story with smithi and drops her at home. Smithi goes to her

bedroom and feels like even she found who is that anand and the relation between them. From that day onwards they meet everyday with any cause and smithi is knowing more about janu and anand relation.

<< *DAYS PASSES* >>

Smithi feels like what to do in her life other than studies. Smithi feels like she is not an ordinary girl to

live ordinary life she always says that she is very lucky to live two persons life in only one time birth. Smithi wants to do something which brings her a special identity. Then smithi thinks to write a book, she shares her thoughts with Anand says it is very good idea but he questioned what genre is the book is? smithi says, it is very suspense and it is futher shown.

"Name of the book is janu. The book is all about the janu biography" Anand been very thnakful to smithi for writing about janu and making her feel like alive in hearts.